Bolton

Pirate Parrot
and the
Knit-wits

'Pirate Parrot and the Knit-wits'
An original concept by Steve Howson
© Steve Howson

Illustrated by Daniel Limon (Beehive Illustration)

Published by MAVERICK ARTS PUBLISHING LTD
Studio 3A, City Business Centre, 6 Brighton Road,
Horsham, West Sussex, RH13 5BB
© Maverick Arts Publishing Limited January 2019
+44 (0)1403 256941

A CIP catalogue record for this book is available at the British Library.

ISBN 978-1-84886-394-1

www.maverickbooks.co.uk

White

This book is rated as: White Band (Guided Reading)

Pirate Parrot
and the
Knit-wits

By **Steve Howson**
Illustrated by **Daniel Limon**

Chapter 1

Everything was calm on board Captain Ken's pirate ship, *The Crooked Cross-stitch*. All the pirates were busy knitting and sewing and stitching.

Captain Ken's parrot, Jim Squawkins, was bored. He and Clarence the ship's cat, Bogey the crow and all the ship's mice longed for an adventure. They were all much braver than the pirates.

A gentle breeze began to blow, and the ship started to rock. All the cowardly pirates turned green.

"It's getting a bit choppy, lads," called Captain Ken. "Head for your hammocks, me hearties!"

Quick as a flash, the pirates ran for their beds.

"At last," croaked Jim Squawkins, "time for some action. Bogey, keep a look-out. Clarence, load the cannon. Seagulls, steer the wheel. Mice, put up the sail."

As they worked, the animals sang together:

"We're fearless creatures all at sea.

We dream that one day we'll be free,

To seek our fortune, gold and jewels,

Without those blubber-headed fools."

Chapter 2

The Crooked Cross-stitch sailed quickly through the waves. From his look-out post high above, Bogey cawed out: "Ship ahoy, me beasties. And it's a pirate ship, full of proper pirates!"

The animal crew cheered as they spotted the great black ship.

"Fearless friends," squawked Jim. "Let's show our shipmates what real pirating is all about!"

The Crooked Cross-stitch sailed closer to the
huge black ship with its tattered black sails.
The crew of snarling pirates stared in surprise
at the ship full of animals and birds. The blue-
bearded pirate captain howled with laughter at
the sight.

"Just look at this!" he bellowed. "The circus has come to see us. What have you motley creatures got to say for yourselves?"

"ATTACK!" cried Jim.

"What did he say?" said the pirate captain, amazed. But his crew didn't have time to answer. The animals swarmed onto the ship. With a meow and a squeak, a squawk and a caw, the brave beasts flung themselves at the puzzled pirates.

The seagulls pecked the pirates' noses and pulled the swords out of their hands. Clarence the cat scratched and spat. The mice ran up the pirates' trouser legs. Bogey the crow went in search of treasure.

Grasping his cutlass, brave Jim Squawkins battled the blue-bearded captain. The angry pirate stabbed with his sword, but Jim fluttered just out of reach.

Jim forced the pirate captain backwards onto the gang plank. The big bad pirate stumbled and wobbled. He took another step back – and dropped like a stone into the sea.

When they saw their leader had gone, the rest of the pirate crew panicked and jumped overboard.

Jim and his animal crew carried the pirates' treasure onto *The Crooked Cross-stitch*. With a yell of victory, the animals sailed away, leaving the pirates splashing about in the waves.

Chapter 3

When Captain Ken finally dared to creep out of his cabin, he found the ship piled high with gold and jewels. The sight of all that stolen treasure sent him into a panic.

"Oh, shiver me timbers," he wailed. "Now every pirate on the planet will be after us! Head back to your beds, me hearties."

Parrot Squawkins knew they had to hide the treasure – and fast.

They set off for a desert island where their old pal, Jack Sparrowlegs, lived.

When they got to the island, a tall white stork strutted out to greet them. It was Jack. He jigged his long legs at the sight of all the treasure.

"Welcome ashore," he called. "I see you've brought some goodies for our collection."

Jim and his crew dragged the loot to a huge nest full of eggs in the centre of the island.

Jack Sparrowlegs lifted the nest. There was a door underneath.

It creaked open to reveal a hidden cave full of jewels and gold. The animals tipped their new treasure into the cave. Jack shut the door, and put the nest back in place.

"Thank you, my friend," said Jim. "We always know where to find our treasure when we need it."

Jack snapped his beak in delight.

"Eggs marks the spot," he cackled.

Chapter 4

When the *The Crooked Cross-stitch* set sail again, the sky was full of black clouds and an angry wind started to howl.

Captain Ken's crew ran back to their beds as the ship lurched and rolled through the swirling sea. Soon a wild storm was raging, and Jim and his animal crew struggled to keep control.

"Be brave, me beasties," screeched Jim, as huge waves crashed over the deck.

Suddenly, the ship stopped, flinging the animals across the deck and hurling the pirates from their beds.

There was a sickening **CRR-ACK** from below.

"It's a rock!" called Bogey. "We've hit a rock!"

Cold seawater flooded into the pirates' cabin. The pirates ran around trying to rescue their knitting as the ship tilted to one side.

Quick-thinking Jim and his crew untied the lifeboat and jumped in. The seagulls carried the mice into the boat. Captain Ken called out: "Wait for us!"

The ship began to sink, just as Ken and his crew scrambled into the lifeboat.

With a gurgling, sucking, creaking sound, *The Crooked Cross-stitch* disappeared under the waves.

Captain Ken and his miserable pirates sat in a soggy heap.

"We're all doomed!" blubbered Ken.

Clarence the cat snarled. "Do we have to share a boat with these lily-livered layabouts?" he asked.

"Not for long," squawked Jim. "I have an idea. I think these pirates may be good for something after all!"

He flew over to Captain Ken and whispered his plan into the pirate's ear. Luckily the pirates took their knitting needles and wool everywhere.

They quickly got to work and before you could say 'yo-ho-ho' they had made a fine new sail for the lifeboat.

Soon the sail was billowing in the wind, and the little boat set off across the waves.

Chapter 5

The pirates and their beastly shipmates bobbed about on the ocean for many days and nights.

Then one morning, while they were all dozing, there came a **CRUNCH!**

The boat had run aground on a beautiful white beach. Captain Ken leaped ashore, and the pathetic pirates tumbled out after him. They lay in the sand, whimpering with joy.

"This is the place for us, boys," wailed Ken.
"We'll never set foot in a boat again."

"Come on, crew!" squawked Jim. "Let's leave
these lazy landlubbers behind once and for all.

We'll build ourselves a new ship and be proper pirates at last."

A month later, the sandy beach was full of holidaymakers. They were lounging in the sun, digging in the sand and splashing in the sea.

The pirates were happy at last. They were selling knitted swimming costumes, giving donkey rides and serving ice creams.

Captain Ken was putting on a pirate Punch and Judy show using his new handmade puppets.

The only thing that worried the pirates these days was the thought of getting their feet wet.

There was a sound of squawking and screeching.

Everyone looked up.

A brightly coloured pirate ship sailed into view. On the side of the ship was the name *The Beastly Buccaneer*.

Seagulls flapped around the sails. The ship's cat sat grinning on the deck. The rigging was full of scurrying mice and a crow perched on the highest mast.

Sitting at the front of the ship, holding a cutlass and squawking loudly, was a green and red parrot.

It was Captain Jim Squawkins, setting off at last for new adventures with his crew. As they drifted away, the beastly pirates sang out loud:

"We're fearless creatures, off to sea!
At last our dream came true – we're free,
To seek our fortune, gold and jewels,
Without those blubber-headed fools."

The End

Book Bands for Guided Reading

The Institute of Education book banding system is a scale of colours that reflects the various levels of reading difficulty. The bands are assigned by taking into account the content, the language style, the layout and phonics. Word, phrase and sentence level work is also taken into consideration.

Maverick Early Readers are a bright, attractive range of books covering the pink to white bands. All of these books have been book banded for guided reading to the industry standard and edited by a leading educational consultant.

To view the whole Maverick Readers scheme, visit our website at

www.maverickearlyreaders.com

Or scan the QR code above to view our scheme instantly!